In my
ROOM

BY
JOEL BIGGS

ILUSTRATED BY
HAMEDMTN

STUDY
In my room

STUDY
Is where I am king

In my room

I can jump and sing

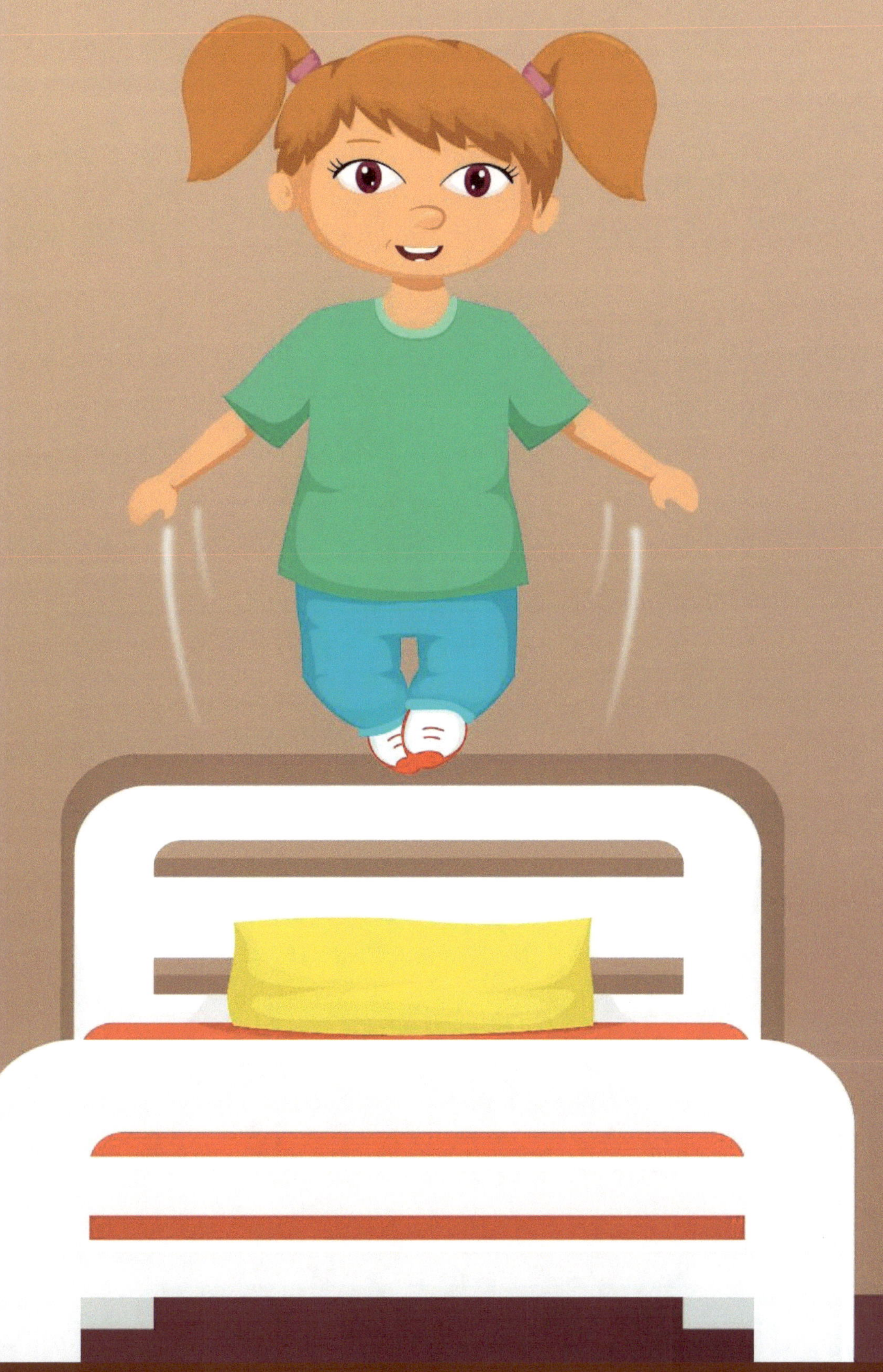

In my room

It's my
special place

In my room

I can fly to outer space

In my room

The sun comes in
and greets me every day

In my room

I can sit and think or
with my toys I can play

In my room

My stuffed animals
listen to me

In my room

I'm anyone
I want to be

In my room

I can build
a fort, a place
where I can hide

In my room

I can climb
a mountain with my
teddy bear at my side

In my room

I can dance or even
stand on my head

In my room

I can touch the sky
just by jumping
on my bed

In my room

I can explore the
world or I can even fly

STU

In my room

I never fail because I'm never afraid to try
VICTORY

In my room

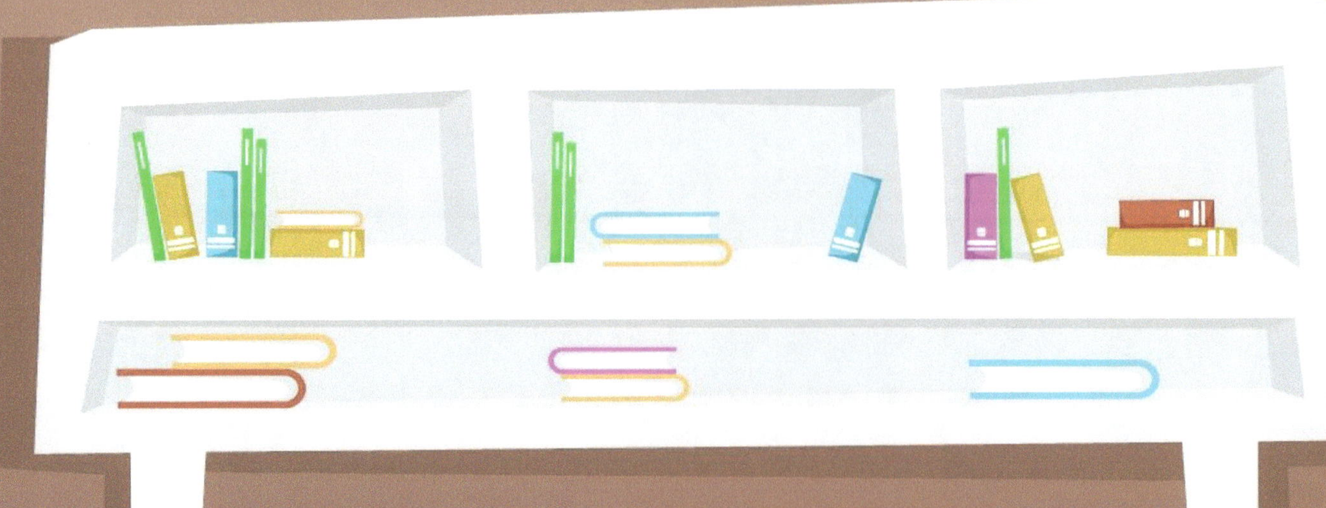

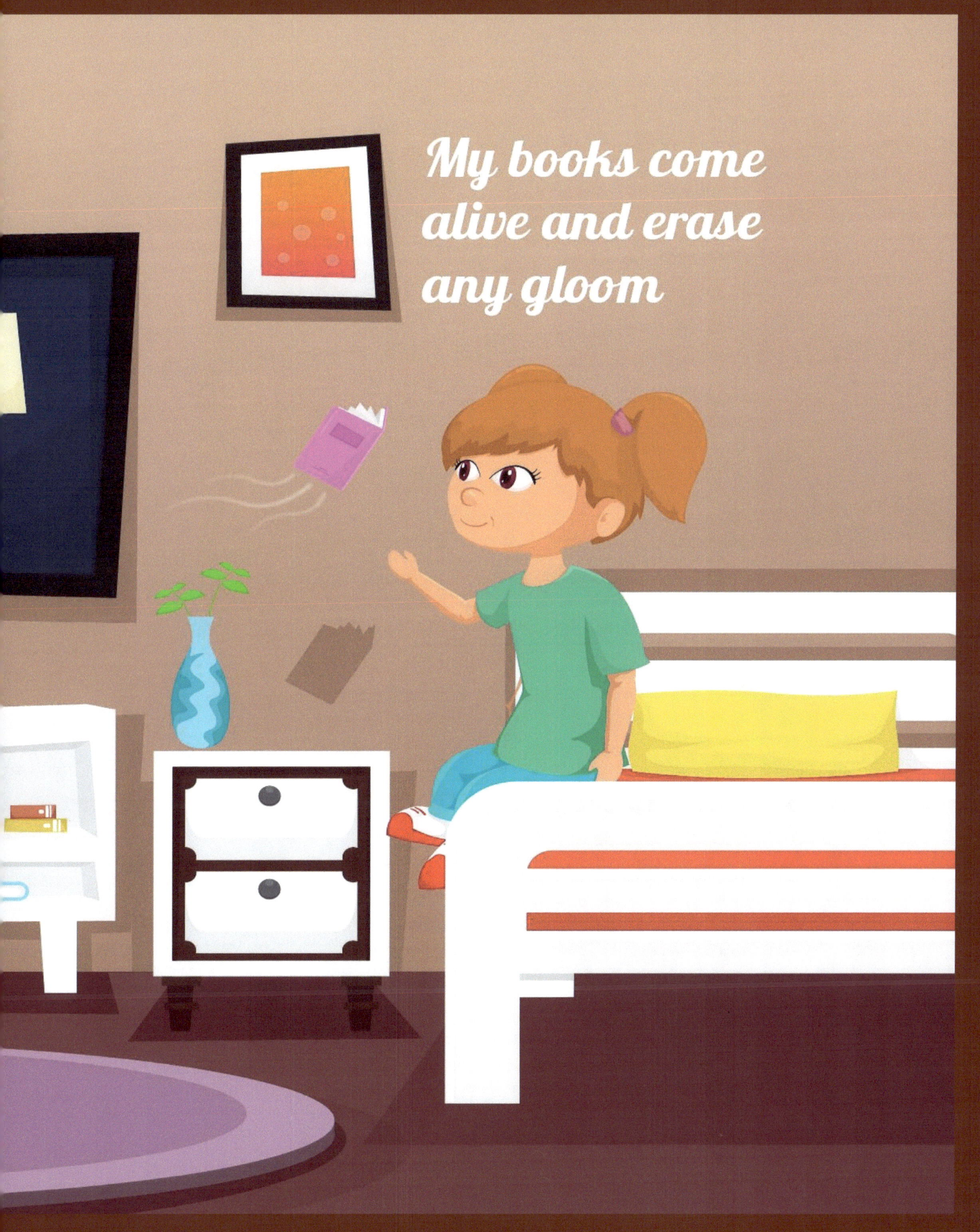
My books come
alive and erase
any gloom

It's one my
favorite places

Being
in my room

www.ingramcontent.com/pod-product-compliance
Lightning Source LLC
Chambersburg PA
CBHW042013110726
48006CB00004B/1073